TWIN TROUBLE

by Luke David

illustrated by Barry Goldberg

Simon Spotlight/Nickelodeon

Based on the TV series *Rugrats*® created by Arlene Klasky, Gabor Csupo, and Paul Germain as seen on NICKELODEON®

SIMON SPOTLIGHT
An imprint of Simon & Schuster Children's Publishing Division
1230 Avenue of the Americas
New York, NY 10020

Manufactured in the United States of America

This edition published by Grolier Books.
Grolier Books is a division of Grolier Enterprises, Inc.

ISBN 0-7172-8910-9

"Give me that rattle, Phillip!" yelled Lil. She gritted her teeth.

"No, Lillian. It's MINE!" yelled Phil. He curled his lip and snarled at his twin sister.

"Is not, Phillip!" said Lil. "The rattle is MINE!" Lil pulled with all her might. Phil pulled with all his might. The rattle went flying to the other side of the room.

"WAAAAAAAAGH!" wailed Lil.

"WAAAAAAAAGH!" wailed Phil.

"Holy smokes!" said Betty, picking up her twins. "I know my pups like to bark, but . . ."

Lil reached across her mom to pinch Phil. Phil reached over to pinch Lil back.

"WAAAAAAAAGH!" both twins screeched at once.

"That's it," said Betty. She dragged Phil away from Lil and gave him to Didi.

"They do seem awfully unhappy," said Didi. "I heard a Lipschitz audio-sleep-tape on twins the other night. He suggests treating twins as individuals for their greater well being."

"For once that old windbag might have a point," said Betty. "We *have* been acting like the twins are attached at the hip. Maybe that's what's eating them. Come to think of it, Howard dressed Phil in Lil's clothes yesterday and vice versa. We didn't even notice until bathtime."

"Oh, dear," said Didi. "Y'know, Lucy Carmichael dropped a bag of hand-me-downs off the other day. Maybe you can find some outfits in there that encourage each twin's individuality."

Betty changed the twins' clothes. "Bingo!" she said.

"Interesting choices, Betty," said Didi. "You're defying gender stereotypes by encouraging imaginative play in Phil and professional aspirations in Lil!"

"Yep," agreed Betty. "These new togs are just the ticket."

“And no more two-for-one toy sales for us!” said Betty. She handed Lil a dump truck and Phil a baby doll. “It’s different toys for you two from here on in!”

“Oh, brother!” said Lil to Phil.

"And now for the final stage in my game plan: separation!" continued Betty. "Deed, you take Phil upstairs, and Stu will take Lil down to the basement!"

“Well, all right, Betty,” answered Didi, “but I’m afraid the twins will miss each—”

Betty checked her watch. “Gotta go. Time for my power swim around the lake. See ya!”

"WAAAAAAAAGH!" cried Lil to Chuckie. "I miss Phillip."
"It's all right, Lil," said Chuckie. "Just pretend I'm Phil."
"Face it, Chuckie," said Lil. "You're not even a teensy bit like Phillip. I miss my twin brother!"

"WAAAAAAAAGH!" cried Phil, up in Tommy's room. "I miss Lillian."

"It's okay, Phil," said Tommy. "Just pretend I'm Lil. Whaddya say we eat these dust bunnies?" Tommy popped a dust bunny into his mouth. "Plegh!" He spit it out.

"No, Tommy," said Phil. "If you want to be like Lillian, you gotta swallow it." Phil popped a dust bunny into his mouth, chewed it and gulped. "Num-num!"

"WAAAAAAAAGH!" cried Phil to Tommy. "I still miss Lillian."

"Don't worry, Phil," said Tommy. "I have a plan." Tommy picked up his cup and string phone. "Come in, Lil! Come in, Chuckie. Over and out!"

"This is ground control, Major Tommy," answered Chuckie.

"We gots to get these twins back together," said Tommy. "Make a break for it and rendez-moo in the kitchen in oh-five-jillion-seconds."

"Copy," answered Chuckie. "Over and out."

"These stairs are too steep and scary to climb," said Chuckie.

"I gots to get back to Phillip," said Lil. "We gots to figure out a way!"

"Lil, Chuckie," said Stu, "do me a favor and wait here while I run Dil's new and improved Kangaroo up to the kitchen."

"Eureka!" said Lil.

"Drat! My dad's new high-security stair-gate is up!" said Tommy. "But don't worry, Phil. I have a plan!"

“Funny, this basket seems heavier than usual,” said Didi as she lugged the laundry downstairs.

All the babies met in the living room.
"Lillian!" yelled Phil.
"Phillip!" yelled Lil.

"Nothin' seems any fun without you," said Phil.
"Being a twin is a prettyful thing," said Lil.

"We tried to keep them separated," explained Didi, "but they do seem happier together."

"Well, you know what I've always said," said Betty. "When twins are happy, everyone is happy."

THE END

Now flip this book over to start another Rugrats adventure.

"You know what, Tommy?" said Chuckie. "It wasn't that bad after all. Glasses make everything look better!"

"And now for the fun part, Chuckie," said his dad. "You get to pick out your own frames!"

"Chuckie, I'm so proud of you! You were a brave boy during that eye exam," said Chas. "And, Tommy, thanks so much for helping Chuckie."

"You did really well, Chuckie!" said the doctor. "The good news is that you're going to get an extra pair of eyes. They're called glasses, and lots of people wear them. Now, would you and your friend like lollipops?"

“Okay, see this cool machine? It’s like a pair of binoculars, but nstead of looking at something far away, we use it to look at eyes up close,” explained Dr. Pedop. “You try it on your friend, Chuckie, and then I’ll try it on you.”

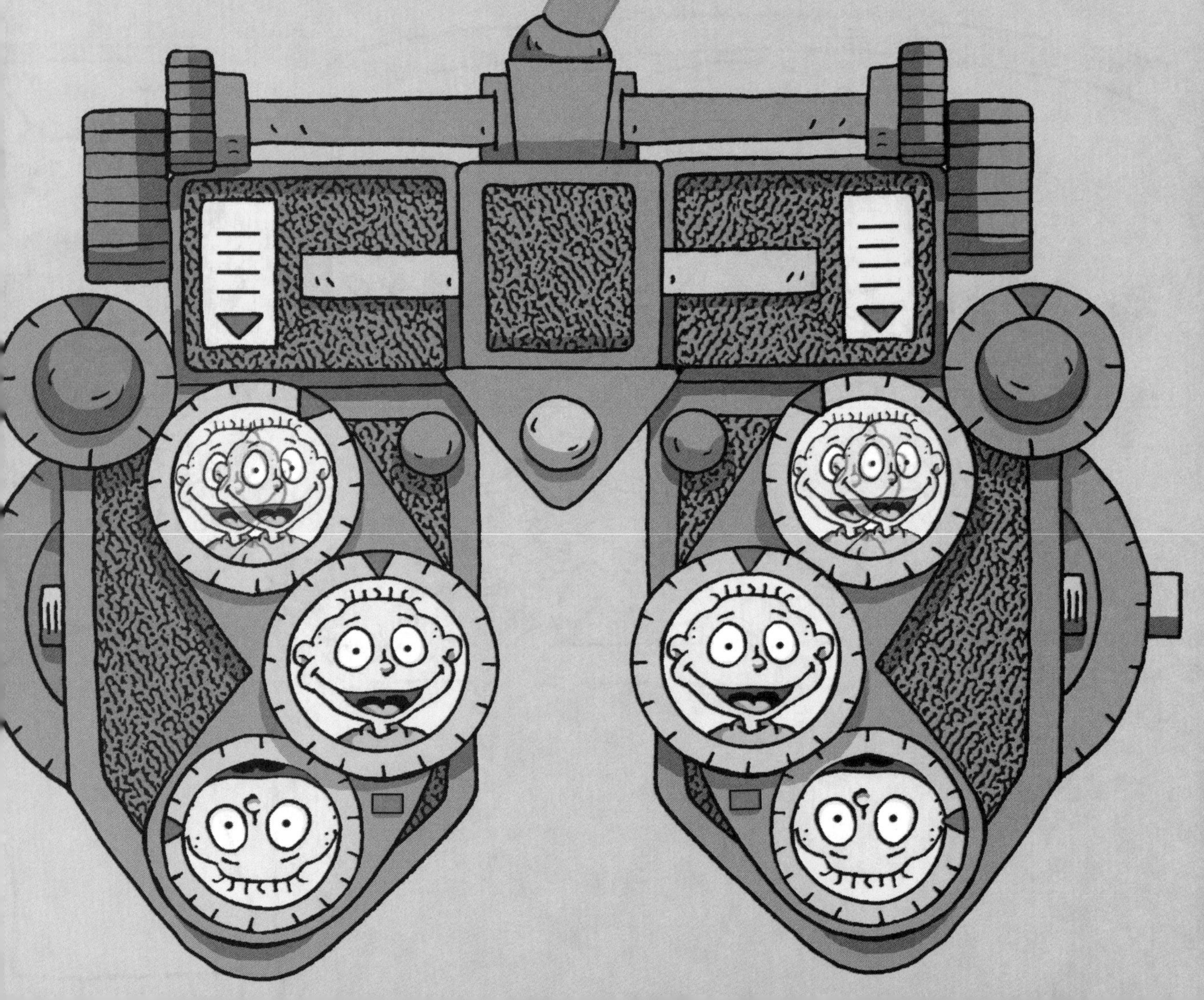

"Now, Chas, you read the chart," said Dr. Pedop. "I'll point to one of these big E's and you use your finger to show me which way it's pointing."

"Now it's your turn, Chuckie."

"Okay, Chuckie," continued the doctor, "you and Tommy can try the lights on each other." Tommy and Chuckie zapped the lights on each other's face. They giggled.

"Now I'll try it on you, Chuckie," said the doctor.

"It doesn't hurt at all, Tommy," whispered Chuckie.

“Nice to meet you, Chuckie,” said Dr. Pedop. “You can sit here, right between your dad and your friend.”

“See!” whispered Tommy. “She looks nice.”

“First let’s test your dad’s eyes,” Dr. Pedop beamed a tiny flashlight right into one of Chas’s eyes, then into the other. Chas smiled.

"The eye doctor can squeeze us in this afternoon, Chuckie," said Chas. "Don't worry, son. Wearing glasses isn't so bad. Lots of people do. I do and so does Tommy's Grandpa."

"Conflabbit!" said Grandpa Lou. "I feel like a human windshield wiper. Why, it took me fifteen years to get used to wearing glasses."

"Don't mind him, Chuckie," said Chas. "It's fun to wear glasses. They help you see everything better. Didi, is it okay if Tommy comes with us to make Chuckie more comfortable?"

"Of course," said Didi. "It will be educational for Tommy."

"TOMMY!" said Chuckie. "The regular doctor is bad enough. Just think how scary an eye doctor must be!"

"It might not be so bad, Chuckie," said Tommy. "Remember how I didn't want to get my rooster shot, but then in the end it didn't hurt at all, and the doctor gave me a lollipop?"

"Maybe your rooster shot didn't hurt, but mine scared the poop out of me!" said Chuckie.

Chas picked Chuckie up and hugged him. "Poor little guy! Funny, but that used to happen to me all the time before I got my glasses. . . ."

"Chas?" Didi asked gently. "Do you think maybe it's time for Chuckie to get his own pair of glasses?"

"He was sitting smack in front of the TV, as if he couldn't see," added Stu.

Chas nodded. "Y'know, I was just about Chuckie's age when I got my first pair of glasses. I'll call right away for an appointment at the eye doctor."

Chuckie toddled right into a small tree. *Thud*!

He was knocked flat on his behind.

"Oops!" said Chuckie.

Chuckie could hear his dad and Tommy's mom talking.

"It's awfully nice of you to help me aerate the lawn, Chas," said Didi.

"My pleasure," replied Chas. Then he saw the babies coming. "Hey, Chuckie, come to Dad!"

Chuckie toddled across the grass toward Chas.

"I can't see," said Chuckie. He scooted forward. "I still can't see too well," he said. He scooted forward again. "That's better." Chuckie was sitting smack in front of the screen.

"Whoa now, buddy," said Stu. "You're too close." He picked Chuckie up and moved him back. Chuckie started to cry.

"Aw, don't cry, Chuckie," pleaded Stu. "Y'know what? It's too nice a day to be cooped up in here. Let's go outside and play in the backyard."

Then Chuckie tried to tag the TV. *Clonk!* Chuckie tripped and fell. "Ouch!" said Chuckie. "I got a boo-boo on my head. I don't think I like this game, Tommy."

"Okay," said Tommy. "Let's do something else."

Just then Stu walked in. "*Dummi Bears* is on, boys." *Zap*! He turned on the TV. Tommy and Chuckie sat together on the floor to watch.

Next Tommy and Chuckie played tag. Chuckie was it. "Got you!" said Chuckie as he reached to tag an armchair. *Wumpf*! Chuckie bumped into the footstool. "I thought the chair was you, Tommy!" laughed Chuckie. He picked himself up.

"You're still it, Chuckie," said Tommy, giggling. "Try to get me."

One morning a long time ago, Tommy and Chuckie were playing Reptar. “Rrrrr! Rrrrr!” growled Tommy. He held his Reptar at arm’s length and shook him fiercely.

Chuckie held his Reptar close to his face and squinted. “Rrrrr-rrrrr?” he said.

Based on the TV series *Rugrats*® created by Arlene Klasky, Gabor Csupo,
and Paul Germain as seen on NICKELODEON®

SIMON SPOTLIGHT
An imprint of Simon & Schuster Children's Publishing Division
1230 Avenue of the Americas
New York, NY 10020

Manufactured in the United States of America

This edition published by Grolier Books.
Grolier Books is a division of Grolier Enterprises, Inc.

ISBN 0-7172-8910-9

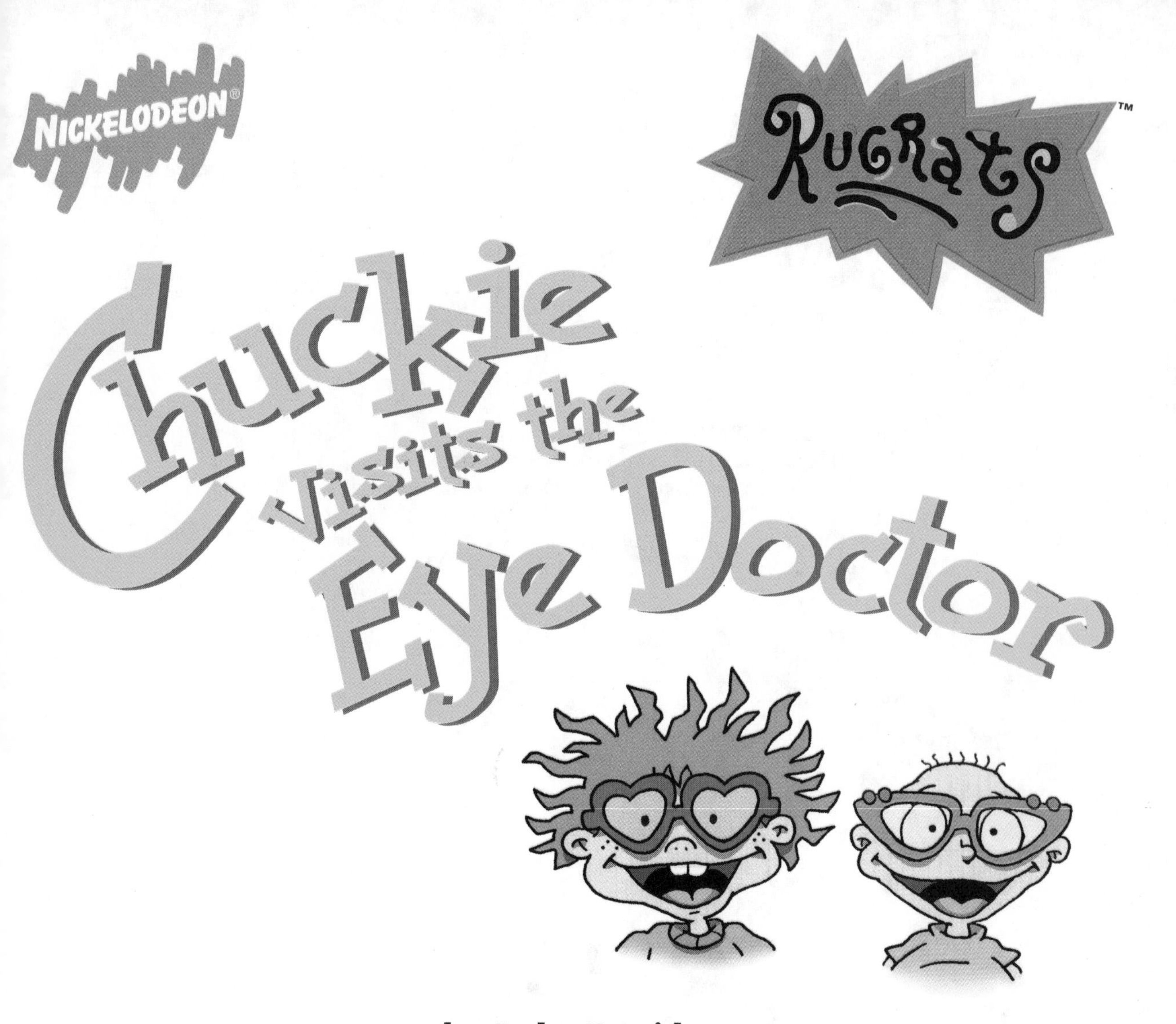

by Luke David

illustrated by Barry Goldberg

Simon Spotlight/Nickelodeon